Once upon a time, many hundreds of years ago, a man called Periander was King of the city of Corinth. Corinth was a large and important city in Greece. Under Periander's rule, the city was peaceful, thriving, and rich, and lots of people lived there.

The King lived in a big palace. He loved music, and he invited lots of singers and people who could play different instruments to come and live at the palace with him. He held lots of concerts, and he was always ready to have a party, and join in with the singing himself.

The King had been told that a man called Arion was the best harp player in Greece. So he invited Arion to his palace to play for him. Everyone was very excited that such a well known person was going to visit the city of Corinth and that they would be able to hear him play the harp.

When Arion arrived, the King held a huge concert. Everyone wanted to listen to Arion play. The concert hall was packed with people. Every seat was taken. When Arion had finished, everyone clapped and cheered, and agreed that he was indeed a skilled harp player.

The King offered Arion a place to stay at the palace. He also offered to pay him well to stay in Corinth and play the harp. Arion was pleased that the King liked his music so much. He was happy that he could stay in the palace and he was also very pleased to be paid a lot. He would be rich!

The King was always happy when he listened to Arion play. He held many concerts in which Arion was the star player. The King hoped that Arion would never want to leave Corinth.

While Arion enjoyed living in Corinth, it was not where he had been born, nor where his family lived. He was also used to traveling around from place to place, meeting new people, and playing at different events.

One day, someone told Arion about a music contest that was going to take place on Sicily, an island to the south of Italy.

He begged the King to let him go.
“I could win the contest! If I do, I will get a big prize, which I will bring back to you, and I will become even more famous,” he told the King.
Eventually, the King agreed. Arion set out by ship to Sicily to take part in the contest.

At the contest, everyone loved Arion and his music. They sang and clapped along, and he did indeed win many prizes. Arion loved the fame and fortune that winning the contest gave him. Everyone wanted to listen to him play.

When the contest was over, Arion needed several sailors to help carry his prizes onto the ship to go back to Corinth. The sailors looked at each other as they carried all of the things down into the hold, where cargo is stored.

"That's a lot of gold, silver, and jewels," they said to each other. "We would be very rich if we owned all that!"

The sailors hatched a plan to get rid of Arion and steal all of his prizes. Once the ship was far out to sea, they pounced on him and told him to give them all of his gold and silver. Arion was very frightened. He offered them everything if they would just leave him somewhere and not kill him.

The sailors discussed what to do.
"If we let him live, then he will tell the King that we have robbed him and we will be in big trouble," one said.
"Yes," agreed another, nodding. "You know what they say. 'Dead men tell no tales!'"

Arion pleaded with the sailors to be able to sing one more song and play his harp one more time. The sailors agreed, so Arion stood up and looked out to sea. He sang, played his harp, and requested that the gods be kind to him and save him.

When he had finished, he jumped off the ship and into the sea below. The ship sailed on and left poor Arion bobbing alone in the waves. Luckily, a pod of dolphins had been swimming by the ship and had listened to his lovely music.

The dolphins swam up to Arion.
"Help me!" he called to them.
They swam around him and allowed him to ride on their backs, holding onto their fins. They took him back to the island of Corinth where he landed safely on a beach. From there, he made his way back to the royal palace and the King.

When the sailors came back a few days later, they went to see the King and told him that Arion hadn't come back with them. They claimed that he had decided to stay in Sicily.

Suddenly, Arion popped out from behind a screen and surprised the sailors. They tried to run away but the guards ran and caught them. The King banished the sailors to far away lands, and they were never seen again.

The King was overjoyed to have his prize-winning harp player back and insisted that he play for him at a huge concert. Everyone in Corinth was invited to the concert to help celebrate Arion's safe return.